For Lara, Maisie and Sophie,
for all of their help.

Ivy and the Lonely Raincloud © Flying Eye Books 2017.

This is a first edition published in 2017 by Flying Eye Books,
an imprint of Nobrow Ltd. 27 Westgate Street, London E8 3RL.

Text and illustrations © Katie Harnett 2017.
Katie Harnett has asserted her right under the Copyright, Designs and
Patents Act, 1988, to be identified as the Author and Illustrator of this Work.

Published in the US by Nobrow (US) Inc.
Printed in Latvia on FSC® certified paper.
ISBN: 978-1-911171-15-7

Order from www.flyingeyebooks.com

IVY and the LONELY Raincloud

BY Katie Harnett

FLYING EYE BOOKS

LONDON – NEW YORK

There was once a raincloud.

(this is the raincloud)

The raincloud was sad because the horrible, hot sun had scared
all of the other clouds away, and he was the only one left.

He had no one to talk to, and no one
to play with. He needed a friend.

So he looked...

...and he looked...

...and he looked.

But no one wanted to be his friend.

He had almost given up when...

...he spied a small figure
down below him.

The girl didn't look happy with the sunshine.
She looked grumpy. Maybe she was lonely too!

So the lonely raincloud followed her
to the market, where she was grumpy.

He followed her to the metro, where everyone was grumpy.

He followed her home, where she was VERY grumpy.

The raincloud was starting to suspect that the girl didn't want a friend at all. But if she wasn't lonely, why was she so cross?

She was grumpy
when she watered.

She was grumpy when
she arranged her flowers.

Even when she
seemed happy...

...eventually...

...she was grumpy.

The raincloud felt sorry for her. Being grumpy is just another way of being sad, he thought.

And then he thought another little thought.

He watered...

...and he watered...

...and he watered.

The next morning the girl
couldn't believe her eyes.

From then on the happy raincloud
and the girl grew beautiful flowers
together, come rain or shine.

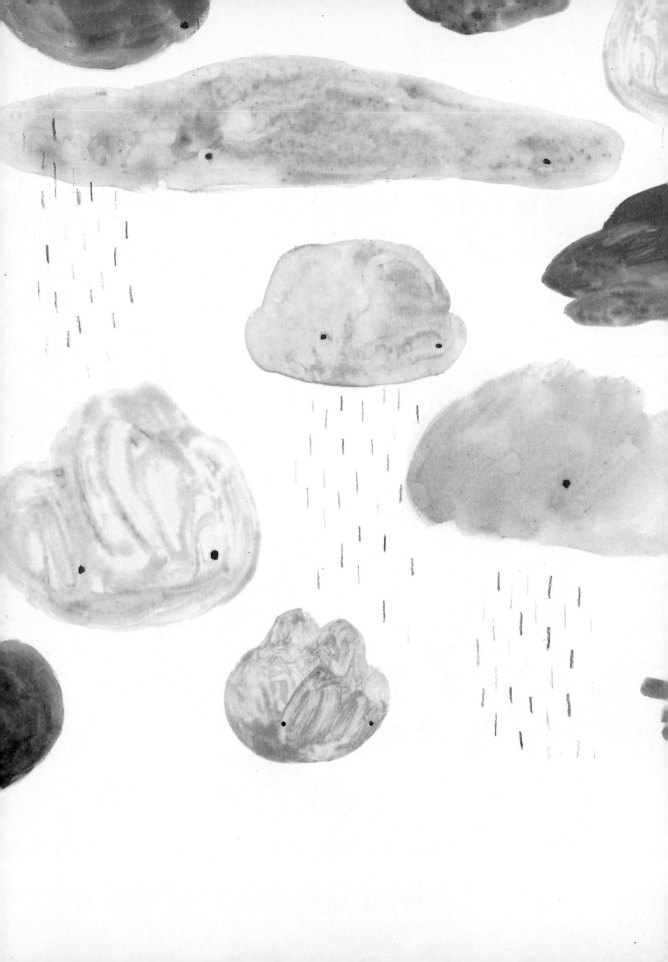